How to be a Practically Perfect Pig

How to be a
Practically
Perfect Pig

nick ward

SCHOLASTIC INC.

NEW YORK TORONTO LONDON AUCKLAND SYDNEY
MEXICO CITY NEW DELHI HONG KONG

For smelly Mel and stinky Nigel

ISBN 0-439-10668-0

Copyright © 1999 by Nick Ward.
All rights reserved.
Published by Scholastic Inc., 555 Broadway, New York, NY 10012,
by arrangement with Scholastic Ltd.
SCHOLASTIC and associated logos are trademarks and/or registered
trademarks of Scholastic Inc.

12 11 10 9 8 7 6 5 4 3 2 1   9/9 0 1 2 3 4/0

Printed in China

First Scholastic printing, September 1999

Have you ever said the wrong thing? Or done something in front of visitors that made your mom turn pink?

Well, don't worry! It's hard to be good all the time.

So let me tell you a secret. From one pig to another. Follow the rules in this book and you will become a perfect pig. Just like me!

Rule 1
Making your bed.

Remember, a good pig will never, ever, ever, ever...

MAKE HIS BED!

When you get up in the morning,
LEAVE YOUR BED ALONE.
Then it will be ready for bedtime —
all rumpled and snuggly and smelly!

Rule 2
Sharing with friends.

If you have a bag bursting
with candy, be a good
little piggy and ...

QUICKLY GULP
ALL OF IT DOWN!

Rule 3

When you need to go!

You may need to go
at any time,

in any place,

anywhere. BUT...

some things are just TOO PRIVATE to discuss!

Rule 4
Table manners.

Table manners are very important, especially when you have guests!

A proper little piggy will always…

GOBBLE DOWN HIS FOOD!

And remember, after you've finished your dinner, always have a great big . . .

BURP!

It shows just how much you enjoyed your meal!

Rule 5

Early to rise.

Ssssh! If you wake up early, and everybody is still fast asleep,

tiptoe downstairs very, very quietly and then . . .

MAKE AS MUCH NOISE AS YOU CAN!

Rule 6

Tidying up.

When you've finished playing…

… and toys are spread

higgledy-piggledy all over the house …

LEAVE THEM WHERE THEY ARE!

Then they'll be ready to play with next time!

KERBOOM

My dad must be a very good pig indeed.
He never puts anything away.

Rule 7
Bathtime.

All good little pigs must have a bath
EVERY DAY. A nice warm bath…

OF SMELLY, STINKY, DELICIOUS MUD!

HOGWASH
Bubble
Bath!

Easy, isn't it? If you follow these golden rules, you will soon become a good little pig.

But even if you forget the rules, don't worry. Mom or Dad will always be there to remind you. And soon you, too, will be a perfect pig. Just like me!

Perfect!

A Perfect Pig Award

This is to certify that

----

has earned the

Perfect Pig
Award

It is hereby confirmed that the above-named piglet obeys all the rules in this book and is a practically perfect little piggy!

Signed

Perfect!

(Mom)